Pup and Hound Scare a Ghost

For Emily, braving a big, new world — S.H.
For Emma, James and Luke — L.H.

 Kids Can Read is a registered trademark of Kids Can Press Ltd.

Text © 2007 Susan Hood
Illustrations © 2007 Linda Hendry

Kids Can Press acknowledges the financial support of the Government of Ontario, through the Ontario Media Development Corporation's Ontario Book Initiative; the Ontario Arts Council; the Canada Council for the Arts; and the Government of Canada, through the BPIDP, for our publishing activity.

Published in Canada by
Kids Can Press Ltd.
29 Birch Avenue
Toronto, ON M4V 1E2

Published in the U.S. by
Kids Can Press Ltd.
2250 Military Road
Tonawanda, NY 14150

www.kidscanpress.com

The artwork in this book was rendered in pencil crayon on deep blue and sienna colored pastel paper.
The text is set in Bookman.

Series editor: Tara Walker
Edited by Yvette Ghione
Printed and bound in Singapore

The hardcover edition of this book is smyth sewn casebound.
The paperback edition of this book is limp sewn with a drawn-on cover.

CM 07 0 9 8 7 6 5 4 3 2 1
CM PA 07 0 9 8 7 6 5 4 3 2 1

Library and Archives Canada Cataloguing in Publication

Hood, Susan
        Pup and hound scare a ghost / written by Susan Hood ; illustrated by Linda Hendry.

(Kids Can read)
ISBN 978-1-55453-142-4 (bound). ISBN 978-1-55453-143-1(pbk.)

1. Dogs—Juvenile fiction. I. Hendry, Linda II. Title. III. Series: KidsCan read (Toronto, Ont.)

PZ7.H758Pusc 2007   j813'.54   C2007-900054-1

Kids Can Press is a 𝒍ⓞ𝐫U𝐬™ Entertainment company

pup and Hound
Scare a Ghost

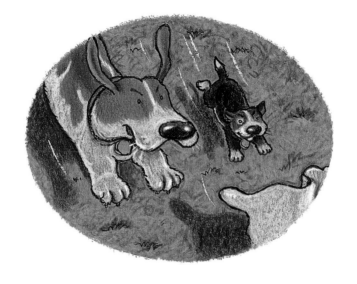

Written by Susan Hood

Illustrated by Linda Hendry

Kids Can Press

What was that?

"Cluck-cluck! Bawk-bawk!"

Who scared the chickens?

Who made them squawk?

Old Mother Hen

was all a-twitter!

The baby chicks

were all a-flitter!

"Bawk!" There it was!

There! By the swing!

"Bow-wow!" barked Hound.

What *was* that thing?

"Ah-rooo!" called Pup,
ready to play.
It fluttered ...

and flapped ...

and flew away!

Dark shadows danced

through the trees up ahead.

Could it be hiding

inside the old shed?

Hound crept to the door.

He heard the wind howl.

His fur stood on end.

He started to growl.

He peeked in the shed.

An owl hooted, "Whoo! Whoo!"

Where had it gone?

Who knew? Who knew?

Peek-a-BOOOOOOOOO!

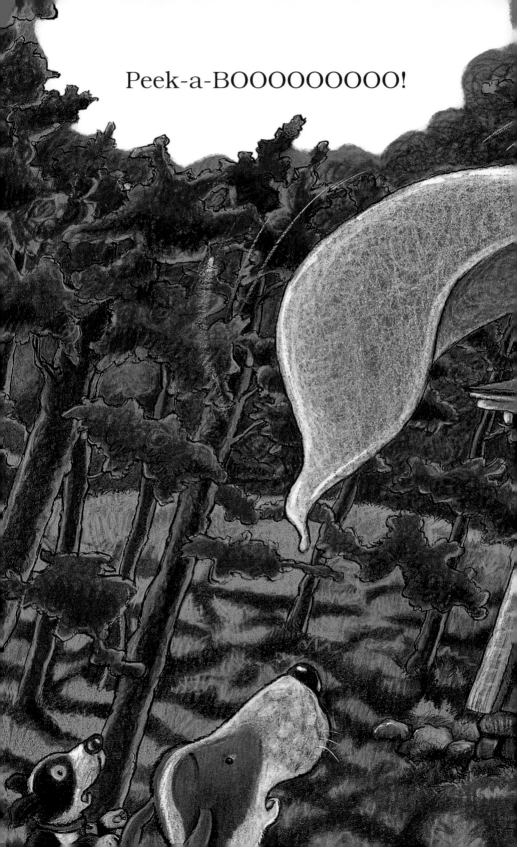

Quick as a bat,

it swooped up a tree.

It sat out of reach

and shook wickedly.

You can't catch me!

it seemed to say.

Then it was up and up

and off and away!

Then it drifted down

and lay quite still.

The dogs crept up ...

and sniffed ...

until ...

19

A bolt of lightning

split the sky!

Whoosh! That thing was off

in the wink of an eye!

Where was it going?

What did it want?

Oh, no! It wanted

their house to haunt!

Pup ran to stop it.

"Grrr ... Yip, yap! YELP!"

Hound knew that sound.

Pup needed help!

Hound found Pup

and a fearful sight!

It held out its arms

and glowed with light.

That spooky thing

was a spooky man!

With a yip and a yelp,

Pup turned and RAN!

The rising moon

made the cornfield glow.

That thing was a sheet
on the old scarecrow!

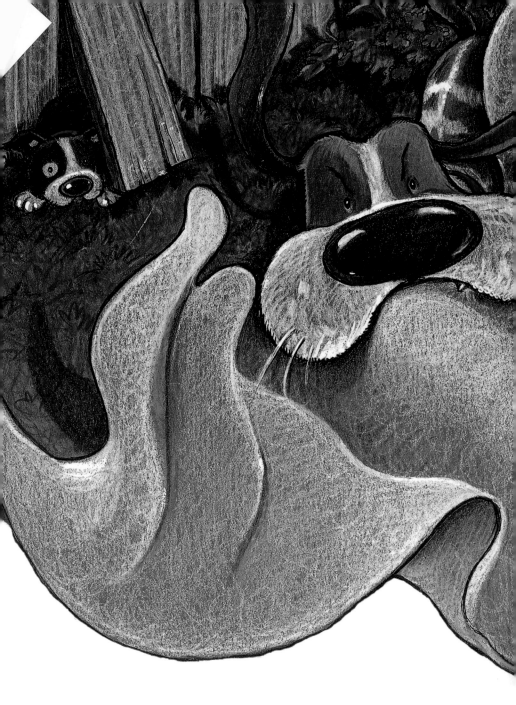

Hound grabbed that sheet
and shook it around.

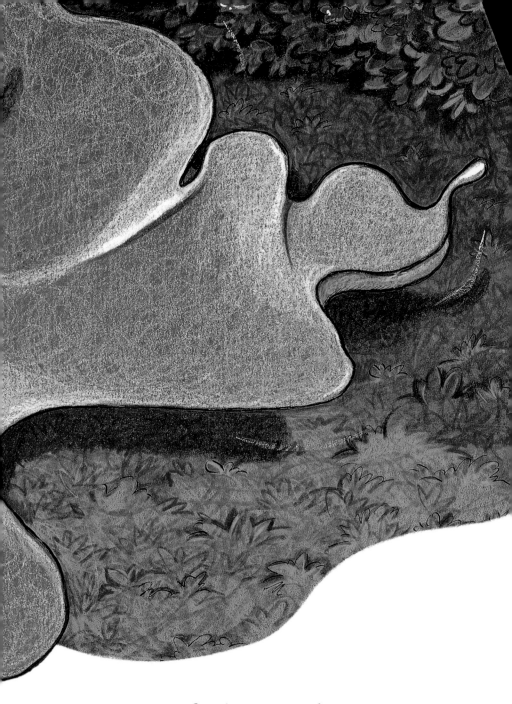

Never fool around

with Watchdog Hound!

Now Pup knows

just what to do

when spooky things

come flapping through.

30

He'll be like Hound

when he grows up.

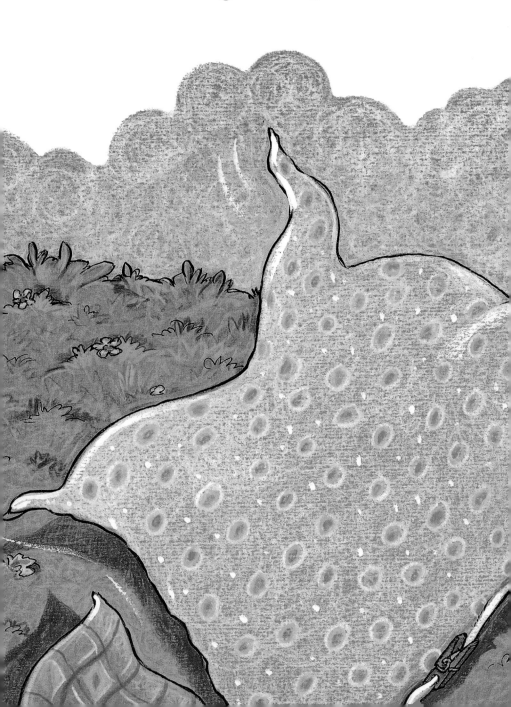

Never fool around

with Watchdog Pup!